FIRST
ILLUSTRATED CLASSICS

The Swiss Family Robinson

Johann Wyss

Retold by Jenny J. Hunter
Illustrated by Barry Davies

After a terrible storm at sea, the Robinson family find themselves shipwrecked on a beautiful tropical island. Together they learn how to survive and overcome the dangers and hardships they face as they struggle to make a new life. Beautiful birds and strange, wild animals all play a part in their adventures. Then one day a ship appears in the bay which may change their lives once more.

Contents

Chapter 1
The Shipwreck

Many years ago my family and I left our beloved Switzerland to found a settlement on a small island in the Pacific Ocean, not far from New Guinea.

After several weeks at sea we were caught in a raging storm that lasted for six days. The ship was blown far off course and the captain was unable to fix our position. At dawn, on the seventh day of the storm, the winds grew more violent, snapping the masts and hurling them into the sea. The ship began to leak dreadfully and the terrified sailors gave themselves up for lost and fell on their knees in prayer, asking God to save them from their desperate plight.

My wife, Elizabeth, and our four young sons, Fritz, fifteen years old, Jack, thirteen, Ernest, eleven, and Francis, six, gathered at my side, trembling with fear. I spoke as calmly as I could,

"Do not be afraid. Have faith in God. He will save us."

My dear wife dried her tears and encouraged our sons to be brave as we all knelt down and prayed together. Suddenly, above the howling of the storm, I heard a sailor cry,

"Land! Land Ahoy!"

At that very moment the ship shook violently and there was a fearful sound of breaking timbers as the ship crashed on to a jagged rock and began to fill with water.

"Lower the boats, men! All is lost!" the captain shouted. Elizabeth and the boys

stared at me in bewilderment as the panic-stricken sailors pushed their way past.

"Try to stay calm," I said quickly and, to reassure them, I added, "We are safe for the time being and we know that land is not far off. Wait here while I go up on deck to see what we can do."

When I reached the deck I was knocked off my feet as wave after wave crashed over the ship. Half blinded by the spray, I finally managed to crawl to a reasonably sheltered spot where I could look around me. It was a frightening scene that met my eyes. Water was rushing in through a large hole on one side of the crippled ship. I saw that a sailor had just cut loose the last of the lifeboats and was pushing off from the side into the raging sea. I realised to my horror that we had been forgotten! We had been left behind with the wreck!

My frantic calls to the departing crew were

drowned in the noise of the storm and I watched helplessly as the boats disappeared from sight. Despite the gravity of the situation I was relieved to see that the ship's stern was wedged high between two rocks which meant that our quarters were above the water-line and, although it was still raining hard, I could just make out the outline of a coast to the south. Afraid as I was, I went below to my family and said cheerfully,

"Things are not so bad. Our cabin is well above water level and we should be able to get ashore tomorrow when the tide turns."

The boys were heartened by my words but I could see that my wife knew we were still in great danger. However, she smiled bravely and said,

"We have a long and difficult night ahead of us. We will need all our strength for

tomorrow so I will prepare a meal. Then we must rest as best we can."

After dinner the younger boys soon fell asleep but Fritz, my eldest son, sat up with us for he, too, appreciated the seriousness of our situation.

"Father," he said, "I've thought of a way of reaching land. We could swim ashore if we had some kind of life-jacket to keep us afloat in the water."

"That's an excellent idea, Fritz," I replied. "Let's try to find something with which to make life-jackets."

In the ship's galley we found several small, wooden barrels which we fastened together in pairs to make six makeshift life-jackets. We were pleased with our efforts and Fritz, who was now very tired, climbed into his bunk and was soon asleep. But Elizabeth and I, fearing the ship might break to pieces, kept watch and passed the long night in prayer.

At daybreak Elizabeth and I went up on deck followed closely by the boys. The wind had eased and the sea was calm again. A bright sun was beginning to rise in the clear sky. We were more cheerful than we had been for many hours. My adventurous son, Fritz, was eager to get started.

"Come," he said cheerily, "put on your life-jackets and we'll soon swim to the shore."

But Jack, my second son, who was a rather timid boy, said nervously,

"I know that you and father are strong swimmers, Fritz, and you can easily manage a long swim, but the rest of us would soon be drowned. I think we should build a raft to get ashore."

"That sounds like a sensible plan, Jack," I said quickly. "Search the ship, everyone, for anything we can use to make a raft."

As Jack opened the door of the captain's

cabin, Turk and Flora, the captain's two large dogs sprang at him. Although the dogs were hungry, they were very tame and licked Jack's face and hands in a friendly manner. Turk even let Jack ride on his back.

"Take care," I said, "hungry dogs can be dangerous."

"Don't worry," Jack said happily, "we are good friends. Flora and Turk will be a great help with hunting when we get ashore."

Suddenly a voice called out from below, "Come quickly! I'm sure we can use these for the raft."

We rushed down into the hold where we saw many large, empty casks floating about. We very quickly hoisted four of them out of the water on to the part of the lower deck that was still above the water-line. I sawed each cask in half, making eight tubs in all. These we placed in a row, then the boys and I found some planks. We set the

18

tubs along one plank and nailed them to it. Next, we nailed the tubs to each other and then nailed two planks along each side of the tubs, thus making a simple, but seaworthy, sort of boat. We cut shorter planks into oars. Then we pushed the boat into the water and floated it out through the hole in the ship's side and tied it securely to the wreck. Our boat was ready to sail! My wife suddenly appeared from another part of the hold, shouting,

"You will not believe it! I've found a cow, a donkey, a ram and six sheep, two goats and a pig! And there are hens, a rooster, pigeons, ducks and geese too!"

"What luck, Elizabeth! They will be very useful," I said. "We will take the rooster and hens with us. The pigeons will be able to fly to land and we will put the ducks and the geese in the water to swim ashore. We will feed the rest of the animals and return

for them later. We must also take food, guns and ammunition, tools and enough canvas to make a tent."

With the rooster, the hens and our provisions safely stowed away in the two centre tubs we were ready to set sail. With Elizabeth, little Francis and Fritz safely settled in the first three tubs, Jack, Ernest and I got into the last three. I untied the mooring-rope and we were off, rowing hard for the shore. When Flora and Turk saw that we were leaving they jumped into the sea and swam after us. A bright sun shone in the cloudless sky and the sea was calm. Helped by the incoming tide, we made steady progress towards land. Many chests and casks from the wreck floated around us and we were able to catch hold of two of them and pull them along with us.

As we approached the shore, we saw that a very rocky and barren coastline lay ahead

of us, whereas to the left the land seemed green and fertile. I decided to try to land there but, before I could turn the boat, we were caught in a swift and sudden current which forced us towards the barren rocks. Fortunately, I spotted a narrow opening between the rocks and managed to guide the boat into the small bay that lay beyond. The water became shallower and before long we touched land. Within seconds the boys were ashore, yelling happily,

"Hurrah! Hurrah! We are safe! Flora and Turk, and the ducks and geese too. We are all safe!"

As soon as we were all ashore we knelt down and thanked God for our safe landing. Our arrival had been watched by a group of friendly penguins and a flock of pink flamingoes whirling high above our heads. We unloaded our boat and pitched our tent near a small stream. The boys collected dry

grass for our beds. I collected dry drift-wood and soon had a good fire blazing. Elizabeth, helped by Francis, began making our dinner. The older boys went off exploring while I went to drag the two casks up from the beach. When the boys returned Fritz was carrying an agouti, a small American rodent, somewhat like a guinea pig, which he had found in the rich, green grass on the far side of the stream. Ernest had found oysters and Jack had killed and brought back an enormous lobster but they had not seen any traces of the ship's crew.

"We will return to the wreck tomorrow," I said. "There is plenty of good grass on the island so we must think of a way to get the animals ashore."

We finished our dinner just as the sun was setting. Thankful to have survived the ship-wreck we said our prayers and went to bed to spend our first night on a desert island.

Chapter 2
We Return to the Wreck

The crowing of the rooster awakened us
at daybreak and Elizabeth and I began to
make plans for our future.

"I think we should explore the countryside
all around for any sign of the ship's crew,"
said Elizabeth.

"Yes, of course you are right," I replied.
"We must certainly do that first and it will
also give us the opportunity to find the best
place to build our home."

Elizabeth agreed to stay behind with
Ernest, Jack and Francis, with Flora to guard

them, while Fritz and I explored the island with Turk.

We followed a path along the shore hoping to find some trace of the sailors but we saw no signs of them. We were, however, relieved to see a calm sea and the wreck still firmly wedged on the rocks which meant that the animals were safe.

We left the coast and turned inland, crossing the stream at a shallow spot. With Turk guiding us through the tangled undergrowth, we made our way to the top of a fairly steep hill. From here we had an excellent view of the land around. The beauty of the scenery left us breathless. There before us lay forests of tall trees of every hue and kind, expanses of brightly-coloured flowers, lush green fields of grass and sugar cane bordering the shore and, beyond, a jewel-green sea sparkling in the sunshine.

In the distance we could see a small clump of palm trees so we went down the hill and walked in that direction. As we were passing through the rich and fertile land we saw many beautiful, tropical birds and several tribes of monkeys chattering noisily in the trees. It was noon by the time we reached the palm grove. A group of monkeys, startled by Turk's barking, scampered up to the treetops and sat there, grinding their teeth and screaming angrily as we ate a meal of biscuits and lobster.

Fritz suddenly had the idea of making the monkeys work for us.

"Watch this, Father!" he shouted. Then he gathered some stones and began throwing them at the monkeys. Although the stones did not reach the treetops, the monkeys were enraged and began hurling coconuts back at us. Fritz, delighted by the success of his plan, laughed heartily and quickly gathered

as many of the coconuts as he could carry. We opened two of them and eagerly drank the milk but neither of us liked it very much. We scraped the white, fleshy lining out of the shells and were surprised to find how good it tasted.

By now it was late in the afternoon so we set off back home carrying the coconuts and the sizable bundle of sugar cane we had collected earlier in the day. We also had with us an assortment of plates, cups, spoons and bowls that we had made from hollowed-out gourds.

On the way back we were involved in a second scuffle with monkeys. We had just entered a small copse when we suddenly came upon a band of monkeys resting beneath the trees.

Without warning, Turk dashed amongst them barking furiously and, before we could stop him, he had seized one of the females who had her baby in her arms.

"Stop, Turk! No! No!" yelled Fritz racing after him. But he was too late. Turk had killed the mother and begun to eat the carcass. The terrified baby monkey, who was hiding in the long grass, suddenly jumped on to Fritz's shoulder and clung to him.

"Father, please may I take him home?" Fritz pleaded. "If we leave him here he will die. I could feed him coconut milk until we get the cow from the ship."

I looked at the helpless creature, no bigger than a kitten, and said,

"Very well, Fritz, since it is our fault that he has been orphaned I think we should take care of him."

We set off home with the baby monkey riding on Fritz's shoulders. The journey passed quickly and we were soon safely back home. The little monkey caused great excitement in the family and he soon became a favourite with us all. When Elizabeth saw

what we had brought back from our trip she was very pleased. She, too, had been busy. She had made wooden spits on which to roast fish and a goose. She had placed oyster shells beneath the goose to catch the dripping fat. That night we ate a splendid supper, finishing with some Dutch cheese from one of the casks we had retrieved from the sea.

"Thank you, Elizabeth, my dear," I said. "That was an excellent meal. We will have to bring the animals ashore before the wreck is washed away. Then we will make our home in that rich and fertile land we saw today. Tomorrow morning Fritz and I will return to the wreck leaving you and the other boys here. Before we leave, I will put a white canvas flag on a pole. In case of danger, lower the flag and fire three shots, and we will return at once."

Very early the next morning we set up the flagstaff and then Fritz and I returned

to the wreck in our tub-boat. After checking that the animals were all well, we loaded six of the tubs with things that would be most useful to us on the island. We took pots, kettles and pans, knives, forks and spoons, casks of butter and wine, sacks of potatoes and grain, sausages, hams, blankets and hammocks, matches, canvas and rope and a selection of weapons and ammunition. With so many supplies stowed away in the tubs our little boat rode perilously low in the water.

"She will be too heavy for us to row back to shore," said Fritz.

"I agree with you, Fritz," I replied. "We will fix a sail and a rudder to the boat."

"And what about the animals, Father? Could we make a raft and float them ashore on it?" Fritz asked.

"I don't think that would work, Fritz. Even if we did manage to get them on to

a raft, how could we keep them there? We must think of a different plan."

"I know!" Fritz cried. "Let's make life-jackets for the animals and then they can swim ashore."

"That is an excellent idea, son," I said, after a moment's thought.

We made the life-jackets from empty casks. We made canvas slings which had casks tied to them in pairs; one on either side of each animal. Then we pushed the animals into the sea. At first they sank under water but quickly bobbed to the surface and began swimming serenely towards land. Delighted by the success of our plan, we immediately set off after them in our heavily-laden boat which, greatly helped by the wind in our sail, sped through the water.

All of a sudden Fritz yelled, "Father, look out! A gigantic fish is about to attack the animals."

When I turned my head to look I saw an enormous shark swimming rapidly towards one of the sheep.

"Quickly, Fritz, load your gun! Fire as soon as he is near enough."

Swimming towards the boat at tremendous speed, the shark suddenly veered to the left and attacked the sheep. Fritz fired his gun and two bullets hit the monster in the head. Mortally wounded, the shark dived and disappeared leaving a trail of bloodstained water behind it. We quickly headed for our little bay and were soon safely ashore, together with the animals.

Chapter 3
We Build a Bridge

Elizabeth and the boys had watched our arrival and came running to greet us. They laughed when they saw the animals wading ashore in their life-jackets. The boys and I quickly unharnessed the animals and they scrambled up the beach in search of food. Then, taking a large ham from one of the tubs, I said,

"Here you are, Elizabeth, this will provide us with food for several days."

"How wonderful! And I have a dozen

turtle eggs which I found on the beach,"
Elizabeth said, smiling happily.

Our supper that night was truly magnificent.
Elizabeth placed a tablecloth over the end
of the butter-cask and laid the table with
the spoons, plates and forks which we had
brought from the ship. We had a memorable
feast with ham, omelette, biscuits and cheese.
Before long, the animals gathered around us
to eat the pieces we left. After the meal we
talked about the day's events. Elizabeth
could hardly wait to tell us of her adventures.

"While you and Fritz were on the wreck,
the boys and I went to explore the land on
the other side of the stream. I think I have
found the most perfect place for us to live!"
she declared. "We came upon a little wood
of the most beautiful trees I have ever seen!
There are ten or twelve enormous trees,
each supported high above the ground by
their massive roots which have formed into

giant arches. If we could set our tent up in one of those trees we would be safe." Elizabeth was breathless with excitement.

"My dear Elizabeth, I think we should stay here. After all, we are protected by the rocks and we can also return to the ship for more supplies," I said gently.

"But we have all the supplies we need from the ship," Elizabeth protested, "and now that you have rescued the animals there is no need for you and Fritz to put yourselves in danger by sailing to and from the wreck again."

"Very well," I replied. "We will make our home in the little wood, as you propose, but we will have to build a bridge across the stream so that we can take the animals and all our possessions with us."

We took the boat and sailed farther along the shore in search of wood with which to build the bridge. We found some of the

wreckage of the ship which had been washed up on a tiny, nearby island. We loaded the boat with planks and timber and sailed back to our island. We used the cow and the donkey to haul the wood to the spot where the bridge was to be built. We had chosen a place where the stream was quite narrow and the banks were firm enough to support the bridge. It took us all day to build the bridge for it was a difficult and tiring task. There were trees growing on each side of the stream. With a pulley secured to a tree on the far bank, we eventually managed to pull three long planks into position to form a bridge over the stream. Across these we nailed short planks to strengthen the bridge and to make it safe for the animals to cross. Then we returned to the tent to collect our belongings and the rest of the animals for our journey to the wood of the tall trees.

The donkey and the cow were loaded with

most of our supplies and I sat Francis on the donkey's back too. The rest of the goods were divided among us and we each carried a sack and a gun. Then off we went with Jack and Ernest shepherding all the other animals along behind. We soon reached the bridge and crossed over to the grassy plain beyond. Flora and Turk barked around the animals to keep them moving through the tempting, fresh grass. Suddenly, the dogs stopped barking and began to howl in anguish. Jack and Fritz ran towards them with their guns ready.

"Over here, Father! Come quickly!" Jack yelled. "It's an enormous porcupine!"

I arrived to find Turk and Flora leaping up at the porcupine, their noses covered with blood. Each time they attacked, the animal's sharp spines pierced them again and again. Very quickly, Jack took aim with his pistol and shot the porcupine dead. The boys were

fascinated by the strange animal which we wrapped in canvas and took with us on the donkey's back.

We very soon arrived at the wood with the giant trees. I, too, was amazed by their size.

"What splendid trees!" I cried. "So tall and grand! Well done, Elizabeth, you have found an excellent place for us to live! A house built in these trees will be safe from all the wild animals."

We had just started to unpack when little Francis raced up to Elizabeth and said,

"Look, Mother, look! I have found some delicious fruit under the trees."

Elizabeth was very alarmed to see him chewing and quickly removed something from his mouth, saying firmly,

"It could be poisonous! Never eat anything if you don't know what it is."

Fortunately the fruit was safe to eat for

Francis had found a supply of ripe figs in the grass beneath the tall trees.

"We shall need a ladder to reach the tall branches of our splendid trees," I said to the boys.

"We could make a strong ladder from the bamboo canes I saw near the shore," said Ernest. "I'll show you where they are."

We went quickly there and soon had three bundles of bamboo canes cut into lengths about five feet long. On the way back we were startled by a noise in the bushes and jumped back in fright. However, Flora, who had followed us to the shore, darted straight into the thicket. Within seconds a shrill, harsh screeching began.

Chapter 4
We Build a House in the Trees

Fearful that Flora was in danger, we moved slowly towards the thicket with our guns raised. Suddenly, a flock of magnificent flamingoes flew up into the air. Fritz fired immediately and two of the birds fell on the ground; one was dead but the other was only wounded in the wing. As Fritz approached, the injured bird began to run towards the swamp with Flora racing after it. She caught the bird by the wing and held on until I arrived. I managed to restrain the struggling flamingo and tucked it under my arm for

the journey home. With Fritz carrying the dead flamingo and Ernest the bamboo canes we soon arrived back at the tall trees. The rest of the family was thrilled to see the flamingo. After rubbing some ointment on the injured wing to ease the pain, I tethered him where he could stray as far as the stream to wash himself.

I called my family together and said,

"Now we must get busy and make a ladder if we are to build our house in the trees. But first, we need to measure the height of the branches from the ground."

"Should one of us climb the tree?" the boys asked.

"No, that won't be necessary," I replied. "I can use triangles to make a mathematical calculation of the height."

The tree I selected had many thick branches that grew close together at right angles from the trunk and I found that the lowest branch

of the tree was forty feet from the ground.
I called to the boys,

"We need eighty feet of rope for the sides
of the ladder. Fritz, would you and Ernest
measure the rope, please?"

We had more than enough rope so, using
short pieces of bamboo for the rungs, the
boys began to make the ladder. I, mean-
while, had been busy making a bow and
several arrows from two long bamboo canes.
When the ladder was ready I tied a long
length of thread to the lower end of an
arrow and shot the arrow over a branch of
the tree so that it landed on the other side.
I fastened a length of rope to the end of
the thread and pulled the rope up and over
the branch until it hung down on the other
side. Then, with the ladder tied to the rope,
it was easy to hoist it into position and to
hold it steady until Fritz climbed nimbly up
and fixed it securely to the tree. The whole

family cheered loudly for we were now ready to start building our tree-house. We used a pulley, which I had fastened to the tree trunk, to raise the pieces of timber as we needed them.

I had chosen an excellent tree for our purpose for it was easy to nail a floor of planks to the horizontal boughs and, with the floor in place, we were able to fix a balustrade of planks all the way round it. About five or six feet above the floor there were branches from which we hung our hammocks and higher up still were more branches. We draped our sailcloth over them to make a roof and, because it was so large, it hung down over the balustrade. With the tree trunk forming the back wall we nailed the cloth securely on two sides of the balustrade and left the front open as the entrance to our house, which was now beginning to look quite habitable. The open

side would ensure that we had cool, fresh air in our tree-house and, to our delight, we discovered that we had an excellent look-out on to the whole of the area around us; the sea, the beach and the surrounding countryside. By evening, everything was ready for us to spend our first night in the tree-house. I made a table from the planks which were left over and nailed it to the base of the tree. Then Elizabeth called us all together for supper and placed a large, earthenware pot on the table. We wondered what was in the pot but when she lifted the lid Fritz cried out,

"It's the flamingo I shot!"

"You are quite right," Elizabeth said, smiling. "It was an old, tough bird so I boiled it to make it tender."

It was a delicious meal and after we had eaten our share we climbed up the ladder to the tree-house. When I pulled the ladder

up after me the excited children said they felt like medieval knights pulling the draw-bridge up in their very own castle. Indeed, as the days passed, we could almost believe that we were the rulers of our own secret island. One day, after lunch, I said to my family,

"Don't you think we should give a name to our tree-house and to the other parts of the island that we know?"

"What a splendid idea!" cried Ernest. "But which part shall we name first?"

"We could start with the bay where we first landed," I suggested.

"We could call it The Bay of Oysters," said Ernest. "Don't you remember that we found many oysters there?"

"No, it must be called The Bay of Lobsters," declared Jack, "because it was there that I found the enormous lobster."

"I think it should be called Providence

Bay," Elizabeth said firmly. "Then we will always remember that it was our Heavenly Father who brought us safely there."

We all agreed with Elizabeth's suggestion and then we chose names for the other places that we knew. *Zeltheim*, or Tent House, was the name given to the spot where we had made our first home. The tiny island where we had found the wreckage to build our bridge was named Shark Island because Fritz had shown such skill and courage in killing the sea monster in the waters nearby. We chose Flamingo Marsh for the swamp where we had shot the flamingoes. The stream that divided the island was named Jackal River and we called our bridge, Family Bridge. It was more difficult to choose a suitable name for our tree-house. The boys wanted it called Tree Castle or Eagle's Nest, but in the end we decided to call it Falcon's Nest.

Naming the various places brought cheer

to our hearts again and we spent the next few days collecting the remaining supplies from Tent House and transporting them to our new home, Falcon's Nest. We also spent some time exploring other parts of the island. One afternoon Ernest and I went on a fishing expedition in Providence Bay where he hooked a magnificent, fifteen-pound salmon. On the way home, Flora, barking fiercely, rushed through the long grass after a most peculiar animal which jumped away from us with giant leaps. Ernest raised his gun and fired and the strange creature fell dead on the spot. When we reached the animal Ernest said,

"Look, Father, he is as big as a sheep and yet he has the tail of a tiger. He has eyes and hair like a mouse and his ears are like those of a rabbit."

"Yes, Ernest, he is a very unusual animal," I said. "His front legs are short like a

79

squirrel's but his hind legs are almost like stilts."

"Oh, Father," Ernest said miserably, "I've just killed what must be the most extraordinary animal in the whole world. Do you know the name of this wonderful creature?"

"Your wonderful creature is a kangaroo, Ernest. And what a surprise! For kangaroos live in Australia. I believe the famous explorer, Captain Cook, discovered them when he explored the coast of Australia."

"We must think of a way to get it home without damaging its fine, silky coat," said Ernest.

When we had run after the kangaroo we had left the sledge, which the boys had made, at the edge of the long grass.

"I know the kangaroo is very heavy, Ernest," I said, "but we can manage. If we tie its four feet to a pole we can carry it to the sledge."

With the salmon and the kangaroo tied securely to the sledge, we made our way back to Falcon's Nest. I skinned the kangaroo carefully and cut away its flesh. I put some of the meat aside for dinner that night and the rest was salted and put in store. Elizabeth smiled when she saw all the food we had brought back with us.

"Well, Ernest," she said happily, "your enormous salmon and the meat will make a wonderful dinner tonight."

Chapter 5
We Visit the Wreck Again

Fritz and I sailed out to the wreck the next morning to collect more stores. We decided to build a large raft to carry all that we planned to salvage. We made the raft from empty casks and then began our search of the ship. When I opened the chests in the captain's cabin I found that they contained a large quantity of gold watches, rings, snuffboxes and other valuables. I called Fritz in to see them and smiled at his amazement. I told him that the captain would have given them as presents or used them for barter whenever he reached a new land. Then it was Fritz's turn to surprise me. He led me to a cask that lay under the stairs and to my delight it contained at least two dozen healthy, young, European, fruit trees which had been carefully wrapped in moss for the voyage.

"What a splendid find, Fritz," I said appreciatively. "We will plant all these on the island."

Then we found a large supply of tools, implements, wire and sacks of corn; in fact, everything likely to be needed by settlers in a new land. It was difficult to choose what to take and what to leave behind and, by the time we had finished loading, so great was the amount of our supplies that our raft and boat rode dangerously low in the water.

Just before we pushed off from the wreck Fritz threw in a fishing-net and two harpoons which were attached to long ropes. I tied

one of them to the front of the boat in case we spotted any large fish. There was a favourable wind and we moved steadily through the calm waters towing the raft behind us. Suddenly Fritz called,

"Father, I see something ahead. Can you tell what it is through your telescope?"

"Why, it's an enormous turtle floating on the surface. He must be asleep in the sun."

"Steer towards him so that we can get a better view," Fritz begged.

I changed course believing that Fritz just wanted to take a closer look. Because his back was to me I could not see what he was doing but suddenly the boat lurched violently and began speeding through the water.

"For heaven's sake! What are you doing, Fritz?" I cried in alarm. "We shall both be drowned!"

"I got him with the harpoon! I speared him!" yelled Fritz.

I realised then that Fritz had only wounded the turtle and it was now trying to swim out to sea dragging us after it. We were rushing along at breakneck speed when, fortunately, the turtle turned for the shore near Falcon's Nest. As we neared land the boat was grounded on a sand-bank not far from the shore-line. I leaped from the boat to free the turtle and saw that it lay badly wounded on the sand at the bottom of the water. To end its suffering I killed it, one blow from my hatchet cutting off its head. Then we waded ashore carrying the turtle's head on the muzzle of Fritz's gun.

"What have you got there?" asked Elizabeth.

"A turtle," I replied. "He gave us a ride that we will never forget. We will certainly need the sledge to get him to Tent House along with all the other supplies we've brought."

When we reached Tent House I removed the turtle's shell and cut the meat off for our

supper. Fritz suggested that we should use the shell for a wash-basin and went off to clean it.

"Don't be too long," I called after him. "Remember we have one more task on the wreck. We must bring the little sailing-boat ashore."

It took several days for us to reassemble the boat. When she was ready, complete with sails and two small cannon bolted to the deck, we launched her. As we neared the shore we fired the cannon in salute. We named our fine new boat 'The Elizabeth' which pleased my wife very much.

"How hard you have all worked to build such a beautiful boat," said Elizabeth. "Now come and see the surprise I have for you!"

Chapter 6
Exploring the Interior

Holding little Francis by the hand Elizabeth took us along a stony path that led up through the rocks. The little monkey scampered ahead while our small flock of geese and ducks followed Fritz and me at the rear. When we reached the top of a steep climb Elizabeth paused and pointed towards the banks of Jackal River. There was her surprise! A beautifully-laid-out kitchen garden, which she and Francis had obviously made while we were working on the wreck.

"It's quite amazing," I said in disbelief,

"and the most wonderful surprise. How did you manage to do all this in such a short space of time? You must have worked very hard."

"It wasn't a bit hard," she replied. "It is good soft earth here by the river and Francis and I enjoyed the work."

"Oh, yes, Father, it was such fun," said Francis. "Come and look! This is where we planted the corn and the lettuce. The potatoes and sugar cane are here. And we planted the fruit trees over here in this part of the garden."

"I can see that there is nothing left for me to do in your splendid garden," I said smiling at them both.

"Well, I'm not so sure about that!" said Elizabeth, laughing. "The plants will need plenty of water." So, at her suggestion, I made a simple watering system from hollow, bamboo canes which carried water from the stream to our precious plants.

We decided to keep the chickens and pigeons near the garden. Every bird would have its own special coop. I made them from gourds and then I lashed each one securely to the branches of the trees nearby. Elizabeth was most impressed with them and said gaily, "Perhaps you could use gourds to make hives for the bees, too."

Our cheerful mood was suddenly interrupted by a loud shriek. Then Ernest shouted out in terror,

"Father! Father! A crocodile! Come quickly! He's asleep on a large rock!"

"What nonsense, Ernest!" I exclaimed. "Whatever made you think that a crocodile would live on a dry rock so far away from any water? It's unheard of!"

"Well, he's there all the same," Ernest insisted. "Come and see for yourself."

We walked softly towards the rock where the creature lay sleeping.

"Why! It's an iguana! An enormous, climbing lizard," I whispered.

"Shall I shoot him?" asked Fritz.

"No, Fritz, his skin is very tough; see how scaly it is. He could be dangerous if he were only wounded. I think I know of a better way to catch him. Now, keep well back and don't make any noise," I warned.

Then I cut a stout stick, fastened a long noose to one end of it and crept quietly towards the sleeping iguana whistling softly as I went. As I drew nearer I whistled loudly and then more loudly still. At last the creature stirred, opened one eye and raised his head as if to hear the music more easily. He seemed to be in some sort of trance, bewitched by the strains of the Swiss melody I was still whistling. Slowly the iguana rolled over once and stretched himself full length on his back apparently spellbound by the music. I continued whistling, never pausing

for an instant and creeping closer to him all the time. Finally he raised his head again and I slipped the noose over him and tightened it. He began to struggle violently.

"Tighter, Father! Tighter!" yelled Ernest.

But I, not wanting the animal to suffer unnecessarily, drew my knife and killed him with one sharp thrust. In spite of his size and weight we finally managed to lift the iguana on to my shoulders. Then, with the boys supporting the long tail behind, we made our way home to Falcon's Nest.

It was almost dark by the time we reached Falcon's Nest. After I had skinned the iguana and cut off some of its flesh, Elizabeth made a meal which was really quite delicious. As we sat beneath the fig tree I said quietly,

"Tomorrow we will sink the wreck and, with luck, the tide will wash the wreckage ashore. We will be able to collect the timber quite easily and to store it for future use.

We must also do some more exploring, especially the interior of the island, for there is much we have not yet seen."

Then I spoke of my plan to blow up the ship.

"I will sail out to the wreck with Fritz, Jack and Ernest. We will make a final search for anything that might possibly be of some use to us in the future. When we have salvaged everything that we can, we will place a large cask of gunpowder with a long fuse attached to it in the bottom of the hold. Then we will light the fuse and sail back to the island as quickly as we can before the ship explodes."

We sailed out to the wreck at first light. By the time we had salvaged everything that we could and had lit the fuse, it was almost dark. We left the ship with sadness in our hearts for it seemed to us that we were destroying the one link that remained between us and our own, beloved country.

When the huge explosion came, dazzling red and orange flames lit up the sky and as the ship sank slowly to the bottom of the sea we wondered if we should ever see our own, dear, native land again.

Early the next morning, Fritz, Jack, Ernest and I said good-bye to Elizabeth and little Francis and set out to explore the interior. Grizzle, our strong, little donkey, pulled the sledge which we had loaded with all the things we would need for the expedition – food and cooking utensils, a tent and extra ammunition. Flora and Turk ran alongside as we made our way to the land beyond Tent House. We passed through several forests and I was surprised and delighted by the variety of exotic trees we saw.

"Look, boys, this is a guava tree. Its fruit is very much like our apple. Here is a most useful tree – the candleberry. Its berries can be boiled to make candle wax. How pleased

your mother will be when she hears what we have found," I said cheerily. I pointed out some of the other trees that we could use,

"The milky sap from this type of tree can be collected in gourds. When it dries it hardens to form rubber."

I left a large gourd under the tree and told the boys that I would be able to make boots and shoes from the sap. Then I pointed out a cacao tree. When I explained how its beans could be ground into powder to make a tasty chocolate drink, Ernest gathered as many as he could stuff into his pockets.

We left the woods and climbed a nearby hill in order to study the area. The view was quite breathtaking for there before us lay a rich and fertile valley with the river winding through it and sparkling in the sunshine. To the right was a range of towering mountains. To the left was a wide, grassy plain with clumps of palm trees dotted

here and there and, in the distance, we could see the beautiful shore of a very large bay.

Suddenly, Jack called out in alarm,

"Grizzle! I can't see Grizzle! Where is he?"

"He ran off," said Ernest. "He just galloped into the bamboo forest and disappeared."

"We must find him quickly," I said anxiously. "He could be in danger."

When we reached the forest we found Grizzle's hoofprints in the damp earth. We followed his tracks through the trees for almost an hour before we reached the end of the forest. Ahead of us lay the huge, grassy plain with the great bay beyond. We made our way to the river which we managed to cross without too much difficulty. To our immense relief we spotted more of Grizzle's hoofprints in the wet sand but, to our surprise, there were also many other, much larger, hoofprints which we were unable to identify. We set off again in search of our

donkey. As we made our way across the plain we saw a herd of animals moving slowly through the long grass. They were about the size of small horses and looked somewhat like cows. We were but a short distance from them when I realised that they were wild buffaloes and, although they now all stood quietly with their big, round eyes fixed on us, I knew that we were in great danger. Before I could issue a warning to the boys, Flora and Turk dashed by us and attacked a small, buffalo calf. The startled herd immediately began to paw the ground and move towards us. Fearing that they were about to charge I raised my gun and fired a shot into their midst. To my complete surprise the buffaloes stopped suddenly, turned tail and stampeded away from us to the far side of the plain, leaving behind the young, buffalo calf with its mother, who had obviously been wounded by my shot. Suddenly she turned and charged madly at Flora and Turk.

Chapter 7
Grizzle and the Onager

We watched in horror as the injured, female buffalo careered towards the dogs with her head held low for the attack. Realising that Flora and Turk were about to be torn to pieces, I took aim and shot the crazed animal dead. The boys immediately came forward to examine the fallen buffalo for they had never been close to an animal of this kind before. Then Ernest said,

"What will happen to the young buffalo? Please don't shoot him too."

"No, of course I won't," I said. "I think

we should take him home with us. We have not yet found Grizzle so this little one can take his place. But first we must catch him."

It took us quite some time to secure the young buffalo for he continued to struggle violently with the dogs. Eventually, we managed to tie his legs to stop him escaping while I fashioned a halter out of a piece of rope. The young buffalo fell asleep, making it easy for me to slip the halter over his head. When I untied his legs and pulled gently on the lead-rope he seemed quite happy and followed after us so quietly that we were able to tie some of our equipment on his back for him to carry home to Falcon's Nest.

Our arrival caused great excitement and Elizabeth and Francis asked us many questions about the expedition. They were fascinated by the little buffalo and the two exquisite birds that Fritz had caught on the way back

to camp. The birds were perched on his shoulders – a handsome, green parrot and a fine, young, Malabar eagle which I felt sure could be trained to hunt and kill birds and small game for us. Indeed, Fritz had already started its training by blindfolding it as a falconer would do and also to stop it from pecking anyone.

"Your expedition certainly was a success," said Elizabeth. "The buffalo is such a dear, little fellow!"

"And I like him too!" said Francis. "Where shall we keep him, Father?"

"I will tether him beside the cow. I think they will like each other," I replied. "But first, we must give him some food."

When the buffalo had finished the milk and sliced potatoes that we fed him, to our relief he calmly began to graze with the cow. Then Fritz chose a place for his birds. He fastened both of them to a tree branch with

the long cords that he had already attached to their feet and then he removed the eagle's hood. The bird immediately fell into a terrible rage and tore the poor parrot to pieces. Fritz was furious and wanted to kill the eagle but Ernest said,

"No, Fritz! No! Let the eagle live. I believe I can make him as tame and obedient as a little puppy. I once read of Caribbean Indians using smoke to tame parrots. I'm sure it will work with your eagle."

Ernest fetched a pipe of tobacco, lit it and started puffing the smoke into the bird's face. The eagle soon became drugged by the fumes and stood so still on the branch that Fritz was quite convinced he was dead.

"Don't worry," said Ernest. "He wouldn't be able to cling to his perch if he were dead. He's merely in a trance and will come to any moment now."

It happened just as Ernest had said it

would. The eagle slowly opened his eyes and simply stared at us in surprise. In fact, Ernest's method was so successful that within a few days the eagle was tame and we had also used the same procedure to solve another problem.

Elizabeth had been anxious to have a winding staircase built inside the hollow trunk of our tree at Falcon's Nest because she thought the rope ladder was unsafe. As I cut into the tree a huge swarm of angry bees flew out and buzzed around the children, stinging them all over. Fritz shouted,

"Quickly! Quickly, Father! Try the smoke trick on the bees."

I ran for the pipe and before long the bees were in a stupor, just as the eagle had been. I cut the honeycombs loose and placed them in the gourds which were to be the new hives for the bees. Once the gourds

were nailed in the trees we had an ample supply of honey close at hand.

The construction of the winding staircase took almost a month. In the days that followed we also completed several other tasks. Elizabeth wove fibres of flax into cloth at her handmade loom. The boys and I planted more crops and built a stable for our increased number of animals, for the goats now had two kids; the sheep, five lambs; the pig, seven piglets; the hens had hatched forty chicks and Flora had given birth to a litter of six puppies. We also dug a ditch to divert water from the stream into the kitchen garden and a reservoir.

Early one morning, just as we were feeding the animals, we heard a strange howling coming from afar. We loaded our guns in case of attack and walked cautiously towards the spot from where we thought the awful noise was coming. Fritz, who was walking

ahead, suddenly stopped and began to laugh.

"Well, Well! Would you believe it?" he cried. "It's Grizzle! He's come home to us after all."

As Grizzle drew nearer we saw that he was not alone. An animal which looked very much like him was following on behind.

"Why! It's another donkey!" said little Francis in delight.

"No, Francis, it's an onager, a type of wild ass that roams through the plains of Central Asia," I said. "And what a stroke of luck to have come across such a splendid creature. Now, although I have heard that onagers are very difficult to tame, we must catch her and teach her to work for us."

We all stood very still. Then Fritz, with a noose in one hand and some oats in the other, walked quietly towards the two animals. Grizzle came up to Fritz and began to eat

the oats greedily. The onager moved closer and when it was near enough Fritz quickly tossed the noose over its head.

We returned in triumph to Falcon's Nest, for we had found Grizzle and captured his strange companion, the beautiful onager.

Chapter 8
The Secret Grotto

Everyone was eager to take part in the taming of the beautiful onager. I knew that it would take a long time for her to learn to trust and obey us but we were determined to succeed. The first to ride her was Master Knips, our monkey who, despite the onager's violent rearing and kicking, stayed firmly on her back. I agreed to let Francis try next but I took the precaution of leading the onager with a halter. Poor Jack was thrown to the ground when he tried to ride the onager by himself. Ernest, Fritz and I fared

no better; each of us was thrown from the onager many times. In the end it was Fritz who tamed the onager for, no matter how many times she tossed him to the ground, he climbed back on and rode away again. After a while the onager became gentle and docile. We named her Lightfoot because of her amazing speed and grace and we knew that she would soon become one of the most useful and well-loved of all our animals. Many years later I would recall with pride the times when Fritz and Lightfoot raced with the speed of lightning across the sands at Falcon's Nest.

After the taming of Lightfoot we spent several carefree days adding to our stores for the rainy, winter season was near at hand. Our peaceful life was shattered by the onset of winter. Torrential rain set in, flooding the entire island to such an extent that it seemed like one vast lake. The raging

storms forced us to move from the tree-house because the rain soaked our beds and the wind blew so fiercely that we were afraid of being carried away. We took shelter in the stable with our animals. We were cramped and uncomfortable in our new quarters, for the pungent smell of the animals was over-powering. Added to this, we were choked by thick smoke whenever we tried to light a fire and soaked by the rain when we ventured outside. We endured these dreadful conditions for many long, monotonous weeks, longing for the arrival of spring.

One day, when our spirits were especially low, Elizabeth said,

"I don't think any of us could face another winter in this place! We must find somewhere else to build a more comfortable winter home. I know that we all love Falcon's Nest so we could continue to use it as a summer home."

"I agree with you, Elizabeth, my dear," I said. "But I'm not sure that we can build a house strong enough to withstand the winter storms."

Fritz was reading a book he had found in the bottom of one of the chests. Suddenly, he looked up and said,

"Perhaps, like Robinson Crusoe, we could make our home in a cave."

"That is an excellent suggestion, Fritz. We will look for a suitable cave as soon as the rains stop," I said.

To our great relief and joy the rains ended a few days later. We repaired the damage at Falcon's Nest and set out to explore the rocks along the shore beyond Tent House. We found that our first camp had been destroyed by the winter storms. The wind had torn the tent to shreds and the rain had spoiled most of our supplies. Fortunately our little sailing-boat was undamaged

but the tub-boat was smashed beyond repair.

"We must build ourselves a permanent home before next winter comes," I declared.

Unable to find a natural cave, we decided to carve a home out of solid rock although I was secretly afraid that it could not be done. We chose a delightful spot with a splendid view of Providence Bay and Family Bridge. I took a piece of charcoal and drew the outline of a cave on the face of the rock. Then the boys and I set to work at once with our chisels, hammers and pickaxes. It was hard and disappointing work for we made very little progress at first. Then, as we went deeper, the rock became softer and we were able to cut into it more easily. Encouraged by this discovery we persevered with our efforts and after a few days we had tunnelled through seven feet of rock. Early one morning, Jack, who was working in

139

the deepest part of the cave suddenly called out,

"Father, come quickly! I have pierced right through the rock wall into a big cave!"

We were curious to see the cave properly so I sent Jack to Falcon's Nest for some candles and also to tell Elizabeth about our discovery. We all entered the cave together, carrying our lighted candles. To our astonishment we found ourselves in a spectacular grotto that was so beautiful we could scarcely believe our eyes. Massive crystals of every shape and size hung from the cavern roof, glittering in the candlelight like a myriad of stars in the night sky.

"It's just like a fairy palace," whispered Francis.

Then Ernest handed me one of the crystals that was lying on the sandy floor. I examined it carefully and said,

"What incredible luck! We have found a

salt mine! We will make our winter home here in this wonderful grotto."

We began the conversion of the grotto the very next day so that it would be completed before the winter rains set in. The grotto was large enough to accommodate our family and all the animals too. We built ourselves four rooms – a bedroom for the boys, one for Elizabeth and myself, a dining room and a kitchen with a fireplace and a chimney to carry the smoke out through the roof. We made a stable for the animals with a room at the side to store their feed and our own provisions and equipment. It could also be used as a workroom when necessary. We fitted our rooms with windows chiselled out of the rock and we named our winter residence *Felsenheim* which means 'The Rock House'.

We were delighted to find that there was an abundance of fish and game in the area

surrounding our new home. Fritz's eagle caught many large cranes as they flew over the corn fields and we saw several kangaroos in the sugar cane plantation. There was a plentiful supply of sturgeon and salmon in the bay and huge turtles came ashore to lay their eggs.

One day, as we explored another corner of the island, we saw in the distance a great many bushes that were covered with what looked like snow. Fritz, astride Lightfoot, rode off to investigate. As soon as he was back – with the fluffy, white balls in his hands – he called out in great excitement,

"Father, could this possibly be what I think it is?"

Chapter 9
A Special Celebration

I took the white tufts from Fritz and looked at them closely. Then I said,

"Yes, Fritz, it is cotton, as you no doubt guessed."

Elizabeth was delighted. The discovery of the cotton was of particular importance to her because it meant that she would be able to make new clothes for us.

"Come," she said, "let's gather as much as we can."

We hurried to the field of cotton and before long had collected enough to fill

several sacks. Elizabeth also collected seeds which she planned to sow in the garden at Tent House.

Writing up my journal that evening I suddenly realised that a year had passed. I called my family together and said,

"Tomorrow will be the first anniversary of our arrival on the island. We must not let such an important occasion go by without celebrating it in some special way. Therefore, I declare tomorrow a holiday for everyone."

"The time has gone by so quickly," said Elizabeth. "Is it really a year since we were shipwrecked?"

"Yes, my dear, and God has been good to us for we have survived many dangers and accomplished a great deal during that time."

My excited sons went to bed early for they could hardly wait for the next day to dawn. We rose at daybreak and were soon

ready for the festivities to begin. Then I said to the boys,

"For the past year you have spent a lot of time practising your wrestling, running, swimming, shooting and riding. Now you are going to compete against one another and prizes will be given to the winners of each contest."

Our festival began with a shooting match and ended with an exciting swimming tournament. However, we all agreed that the riding competition had been the most enjoyable event of the day. Fritz rode Lightfoot and Ernest rode Grizzle but Jack, mounted on his buffalo, easily surpassed his brothers in horsemanship for he displayed such skills that even a practised groom could not have handled a thoroughbred horse with more ease and grace.

While I was complimenting Jack on the way he had trained his buffalo, little Francis rode into the arena on the bull calf who had been born in the early spring.

"Watch me, Father," he called, "and see what I can do."

Elizabeth had made a bridle, a little saddle and a pair of stirrups from kangaroo skin. Francis, with the reins in one hand and a whip in the other, began to ride his pet around the arena. We were filled with amazement when we saw how readily the little bull obeyed his young master's commands.

We returned to the grotto for the prize-giving ceremony. Elizabeth, our festival queen, was seated in state on a chair bedecked with flowers. I announced the winner of each event and, as the boys came forward, 'the queen' kissed each one in turn and handed out the prizes.

Fritz received an English rifle and a hunting knife for his success in the swimming

and shooting competitions. Ernest, the winner of the running contest was presented with a gold watch and Jack was given a pair of steel spurs and a whip for being the best rider. Francis also got a whip and some new stirrups for his skill in the training and riding of his young bull calf.

The boys were delighted with their prizes and declared it the best holiday they had ever had. Then I turned to Elizabeth and handed her a beautiful work box containing scissors, needles, pins and a thimble.

"This is for you, dear Elizabeth, to thank you for all the love and support you have given to all of us during the past year," I said fondly.

The next day we returned to work for we were anxious to complete our preparations for the coming winter before the rains set in. Ever mindful of danger we rarely worked alone. One day, however, Jack went off without telling us where he was going. Mounted on Grizzle, he rode to Flamingo Marsh to gather reeds to make nests for the pigeons. When he got there he found that the long straight reeds were growing in the middle of the swamp. As he stepped carefully towards the reeds he suddenly slipped and fell into a patch of soft, black mud and began to sink.

"Help! Help!" he yelled, as the quicksand gradually dragged him deeper and deeper.

Chapter 10
The Terrible Serpent

The more Jack struggled to get out, the more deeply he sank into the quicksand. Hearing his desperate cries for help Grizzle ran to the edge of the swamp and began to bray loudly but no one else heard them at all. Then Jack, in a final attempt to save himself, cut down all the reeds he could reach and pushed them under his arms. Fortunately the reeds kept him from sinking any further and, using them as a support, he was able to make some progress towards firmer ground. He called Grizzle who came

close enough for Jack to seize his tail. Then the donkey pulled hard and dragged Jack safely to dry land.

When Jack told us about his adventure Elizabeth made him promise not to go off by himself again. Then she sent him off to change his clothes and wash himself in the stream.

"You must keep your promise, Jack," she called after him, "and as for the reeds you brought back, we will use them to make baskets for carrying our corn."

We were determined to make further improvements to the grotto before the onset of winter. The one, great problem which we had to overcome at *Felsenheim* was the lack of daylight. The grotto was in constant darkness with the exception of our rooms which had windows. The problem was eventually solved by using one of the lanterns which we had brought from the ship. I cut

a bamboo pole which was long enough to reach from the floor to the roof of the cave. I planted it firmly in the ground and asked Jack to climb to the top, taking with him a hammer, a pulley and a rope. He soon had the pulley fixed in the rock and the rope in position. Then he climbed down again and I tied the lantern to one end of the rope and raised it to the roof. Now we could light up the grotto whenever we wished and, to our surprise and delight, the grotto became as bright as day for the walls reflected the light from the lantern very well indeed.

We set to work to complete the improvements to our grotto and to get the winter supplies for the animals and ourselves safely stored away. We worked hard to put the finishing touches to our winter residence, *Felsenheim*. Elizabeth and Jack put the kitchen in order, Fritz and I fitted out the workroom and Ernest and little Francis

arranged our collection of books on some shelves. We were surprised at the size of our library. In addition to the Bible, which we read every day, we had a great many books on history, travel and natural history which we had found in the captain's cabin. We had also salvaged from the wreck a globe, some maps and several foreign dictionaries. Although we all spoke French and German, the main languages of our native Switzerland, I decided that the boys should also learn English since it is so widely used these days. As for myself, I determined to master the language of the Malays for a study of the charts and maps suggested that we were not too far from Malaya.

We had almost finished our work at the grotto when the temperature began to fall, large black clouds gathered on the horizon and the rains set in. We spent the next few weeks safe and warm inside our splendid

cave and just when we thought the rains would end a violent storm began. Incredibly high winds dashed the sea on to the rocks, thunder roared and the lightning flashed across the sky with such intensity that we dreaded to think what might have become of us had we still been living in the tree-house at Falcon's Nest. Gradually the raging storm died away and when the rain stopped we went out to investigate the storm damage.

We were not surprised that it was Fritz who first spotted a strange creature in the distance for he had very sharp eyes indeed.

"Look, Father!" he cried. "It is near Falcon's Nest on the far side of the stream but it is heading straight towards us. I can't tell what it is but it doesn't appear to have any legs or feet. It moves rapidly along the ground by rolling itself up into large rings then unrolling itself again."

I took the telescope from Ernest and

THE SWISS FAMILY ROBINSON

pointed it in the direction of Falcon's Nest. I could scarcely believe what I saw.

"Run! Run quickly, everyone. It's an enormous serpent," I yelled. "We must get back to the grotto at once for the huge, greenish-coloured monster coming towards us is a giant boa constrictor!"

We ran as fast as we could and locked ourselves in the grotto. We barricaded the door and windows and waited silently for our awesome enemy to arrive. We had pushed our guns through a window and we could see the serpent heading swiftly for the grotto. When the serpent was less than forty paces from us it stopped and raised its head and looked all around as if it knew we were near. At that moment Ernest fired. His shot was closely followed by those of Jack, Francis and even Elizabeth. As the animal turned, Fritz and I also fired several shots but it was clear that none of the bullets had penetrated

its scales. As we watched the monster slither away into the marsh we realised that we were powerless to kill it and that we remained in very great danger as long as the terrible serpent was in the area.

"No one is allowed to leave the grotto," I said firmly. "And the door must be kept closed at all times."

At *Felsenheim* we lived in fear for three whole days, not daring to venture outside. We realised that the boa constrictor was still in the neighbourhood because the ducks and geese were noisy and restless. I knew that to mount an attack would be too dangerous for it could easily cost the life of one of us. By the end of the third day there was no food left for the animals so I decided to let Fritz lead them across the stream to graze in the meadow beyond. Early next morning we tied the animals together, in single file, with a long length of rope. Then I said,

"Now, Fritz, you will ride Lightfoot and lead the animals. I will take my most powerful rifle and find a place on a high rock to keep watch. Elizabeth, you and the younger boys will stay in the grotto but all of you must be ready to fire should the serpent appear."

Unfortunately, Elizabeth opened the door before I gave the signal and Grizzle, spotting daylight, broke free from the rope and shot out through the door like a bullet from a gun. We all shouted to him.

"No, Grizzle, no! Come back!" But he took no notice of our desperate cries and ran headlong into the marsh. At that same moment we saw the deadly boa rise up with its enormous mouth wide open as it darted towards our poor, defenceless donkey.

Chapter 11
The Ostriches

Grizzle started to run the very moment he saw what danger he was in, braying loudly as he went, but nothing could save him now. We watched in horror as the terrible monster stretched out and wrapped itself around the donkey, squeezing him tighter and tighter in its powerful coils.

Elizabeth and the boys cried out in terror and dismay as we watched the deadly struggle.

"It's horrible!" sobbed Elizabeth. "We must do something to save poor Grizzle."

The boys urged me to shoot the boa.

"No, boys, I dare not shoot for if the snake is only wounded it could turn and attack one of us," I explained.

The boa crushed the donkey again and again until, mercifully, he was dead. Then the snake swallowed him whole and it immediately seemed to lose its strength and lay motionless on the ground in a kind of stupor. This was the moment for which I had been waiting.

"Come, Fritz," I said. "We have the serpent in our power at last. Take aim and fire when I fire."

As the bullets struck, the boa raised its head and stared at us with hatred in its glittering eyes. Moving closer, we took aim again and shot it through the eyes. A feeble quiver ran through the swollen body and the monster soon lay dead at our feet.

Elizabeth and the boys came running and we all stood and stared in silence at the

dead snake on the sand. Then Elizabeth spoke.

"Now that we are safe," she said, "we must thank God for his great mercy."

I gathered my family around me and we fell to our knees in prayer. Then I said,

"There is nothing more to fear from this boa but it may have left a mate or some young ones elsewhere. We must make a thorough search of the marsh and the land around Falcon's Nest."

We combed the whole marsh but found no other serpent, no eggs and no young ones. But we did notice several traces of our boa – broken reeds and circular marks in the wet mud where the serpent had rested. At the far side of the marsh Ernest came upon what he thought was a young boa. With great courage he had calmly approached it and killed it with the butt of his rifle. When I examined the creature I saw that it was a large eel but I still praised Ernest for his bravery. We found a few traces of the boa near Falcon's Nest but we saw hardly any signs when we searched the surrounding countryside. Convinced that we were safe now, we made our way back to the grotto for supper. Earlier that day Fritz had spent some time preparing a special meal for us. He had stuffed a pig with roots and potatoes, wrapped it in leaves and bark and left it roasting on hot stones in a hole in the ground. He had covered the whole pig with more hot stones, then he had scattered a layer of bark and earth over it. An appetising smell now filled the air and when Fritz served the roast joint we all declared it quite delicious.

After we had finished our meal we made plans for the future. We had been on the island for two years and there were some parts of it still to be explored.

"We should make another excursion into

the interior," I said to my family, "and, if you all agree, we will leave tomorrow morning."

We set off at dawn and walked for two hours in the direction of the land beyond the rocks. We stopped at the edge of a small wood perched on a high hill overlooking a vast stretch of flat land. After pitching our tent we searched the wood and disturbed two wildcats who escaped through the trees before we could shoot them. We decided that Elizabeth and Francis should stay at the camp while the older boys and I explored the plain. We soon reached the land where we had captured Jack's buffalo. We marched on and, the farther we went, the more dry and parched the land became. We were in a desert; a desert so vast that we could not see the extent of it. The sand burned our feet and the sun beat down on our heads to such a degree that we were forced to seek

shade after about two hours. We rested in the shadow of a huge rock. We were all extremely thirsty but the water in the gourds was too warm to drink so we poured it away. Fortunately I had some sugar-cane in my bag and this refreshed us very well. Suddenly, Fritz jumped to his feet and exclaimed in excitement,

"Look, Father, look! I can see three horsemen and they are galloping in our direction! I do believe they are Arabs!"

"Surely not?" I said in disbelief. "Here, Ernest, you take a look through the telescope."

"They look like wagons loaded with hay!" said Ernest.

"Let me look," Jack begged. "You were right, Fritz! I can see lances with banners flying so they must be Arabs."

I took the telescope from Jack and raised it to my eye.

THE SWISS FAMILY ROBINSON

"No, boys," I said. "They are not Arabs or hay wagons. What you see is a group of ostriches coming towards us. We must hide from them and see if we can take one alive."

We hid behind some large plants that were growing between the rocks and waited in silence until the ostriches were very near. Unfortunately, we were unable to restrain our impatient dogs and they charged the ostriches who promptly fled across the plain.

"Quickly, Fritz, set your eagle free," I ordered.

Fritz deftly removed the hood from the eagle's head and sent his bird after the fleeing ostriches. Within seconds the eagle had brought to the ground a beautiful, male ostrich. We ran to save the ostrich but it was already dead, killed by the eagle's savage attack upon its head and eyes. We took some of the magnificent, white feathers from the

ostrich's tail and started for home. Suddenly Jack called out,

"Look what I have found! An ostrich nest! And there are eggs too! We could take them home to hatch."

The eggs were about seven inches long and I estimated that each one weighed three or four pounds.

"It would be impossible for us to carry them all safely back home. We will take one each and return for the others some other time," I said.

On the way back we came across an oasis with a pool of clear, fresh water. All around it we saw the hoofprints of buffalo and antelope. Refreshed, we walked on. Eventually we came to a beautiful, grassy valley with a river running through it. We decided to name this delightful place Green Valley.

We set off again. Ernest ran on ahead with one of the dogs. Suddenly we heard a dreadful roar followed by Ernest's terrified screams. Then, seconds later, we saw him come running towards us, his face white as a sheet. Trembling with fear he collapsed in my arms.

"Bears!" he cried. "Two big bears are coming after me!"

Chapter 12
We Catch an Ostrich

The huge, brown bears came lumbering towards us. I spoke softly to the boys.

"Stand still," I breathed. "Be ready to fire when I give the signal."

We quickly loaded our guns. Fritz stood firmly at my side, while Jack stood a little way behind with Ernest, who was still trembling with fright.

"Now, boys!" I shouted. "Fire now!"

We all fired at the same moment, breaking the shoulder of one of the bears and shattering the jaw of the other. Then Flora and

Turk began attacking them savagely and within seconds were covered with blood. We were afraid to fire again from our position for fear of hitting the dogs.

"Move in closer and aim at the bears' heads," I said as calmly as I could.

We stepped cautiously ahead, took careful aim and fired once more. The bears staggered backwards and fell dead on the ground. We covered them with thorny branches and went back to our camp for the night.

The following morning we returned with Elizabeth and Francis, skinned the bears and then spent the rest of the day preserving the bears' flesh. We salted and smoked the joints of meat before storing them for winter use. We collected at least a hundred pounds of fat which we stored in bamboo casks. This would be used for cooking or spreading on bread in place of butter. We threw the bears' carcasses to our brave dogs and we gave

Elizabeth the carefully-scrubbed skins which would be used as rugs or bed covers.

Shortly after we had finished dealing with the bears I told the boys that they could make a trip into the desert on their own. Fritz and Jack were delighted but Ernest said,

"I will stay here because I want to make cups from the ostrich eggs."

Little Francis, however, begged to be allowed to go and so it was that Jack and Francis mounted on Storm, our buffalo, and Fritz, on Lightfoot, rode away on their expedition early the next day.

While his brothers were away Ernest made his cups and then helped Elizabeth and me to put the camp in order. It was almost dark by the time we had finished our various tasks. We sat around the fire, where Elizabeth was cooking two bears' paws for supper. Then we saw our young hunters come galloping home.

THE SWISS FAMILY ROBINSON

"We had a marvellous chase, Father!" cried Jack. "Fritz's eagle captured a cuckoo and two angora rabbits! See how beautiful they are!"

Then Francis told us of how the cuckoo, or honey guide, had led them to a nest of bees where we could find honey.

"But that's not all," said Fritz. "We saw a herd of antelope grazing beyond the rocks and we managed to drive them through a narrow pass into our area."

Then Fritz said thoughtfully,

"If we were to put all our new animals on Shark Island we would be able to hunt and tame them more easily and we would have a good supply of food as well as skins and furs to make clothes and hats."

We all agreed that this was an excellent plan and Elizabeth said,

"That is a very good idea, Fritz, for these rabbits, lovely as they are, breed so fast that

soon there would be nothing left in my vegetable garden."

"By the way, boys, did you happen to pass by the ostrich's nest?" I asked.

"No, Father," answered Fritz, "we did not have time for we were too busy with the antelope."

"In that case," I said, "we will go again tomorrow for I also want to collect some sap from the large plants growing there."

We set out early. Jack rode Storm and Francis rode the little bull. I rode Lightfoot and Fritz rode her young colt foal, Rapid, who had been born some months earlier. We went by way of Green Valley and saw several familiar landmarks. We soon reached the spot where we had first seen the giant birds. We had named the large rock Arab's Tower because Fritz had thought that the ostriches were Arabian horsemen.

We were determined to take an ostrich

alive this time. Fritz had already tied up his eagle's beak and muzzled the dogs. As we neared the nest, four superb ostriches, a male, and three females, stood up and moved towards us. We were anxious to catch the male because he was the largest bird and even more splendid than the females. I hurled my sling – a long thin rope with weights attached to each end of it. It fell over the ostrich and wound itself around his body instead of his legs, as I had intended. As the terrified bird ran away Fritz sent his eagle after it. The eagle flew down and knocked the ostrich to the ground. Quick as a flash, Jack threw his sling round its legs and we all cheered loudly for we had successfully captured our magnificent ostrich. Then I tied him between the bull and the buffalo and we returned safely to the tent. Elizabeth and Ernest were amazed when they saw the ostrich and wanted to know every detail of his capture.

We made our way home to *Felsenheim*, unpacked all the things we had brought back with us and placed the ostrich eggs in the oven to incubate. Then we began training our ostrich in earnest. He was very fierce at first, attacking us with claws and beak and rejecting all the foods we offered him. He became so weak that in the end we forced pats of butter and corn down his throat. He tried to spit them out but he grew to like them and from then on thrived well. After about a month the ostrich was tamed completely. He had learned to carry a saddle and we now had a steed that was faster than any of our other mounts.

At about this time, three of the eggs hatched out. The ostrich chicks were the strangest-looking birds we had ever seen. They looked like fluffy ducks but had long, thin legs, like stilts. We looked after the young ostriches as well as we could. Their shells made excellent vases which Elizabeth filled with colourful flowers to decorate the grotto.

Chapter 13
We Make a Kayak

One day Fritz told us of a new project he had in mind.

"It seems to me," he said, "that we have most of the things we need now. The ostrich makes an excellent workhorse and we have a sledge to haul our supplies. We also have a sailing-boat and a canoe at anchor in Providence Bay. However, I think we need a swifter boat – one that will skim over the water as fast as our ostrich runs over the land. We should build ourselves a kayak."

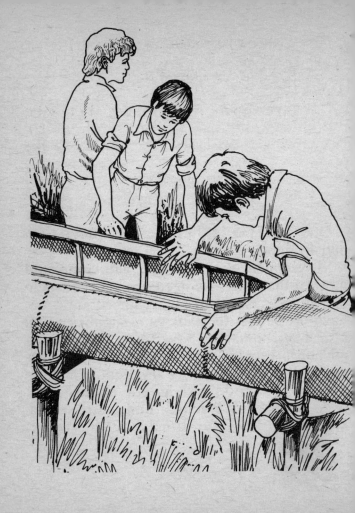

"A kayak!" exclaimed Jack. "What is a kayak?"

"A kayak is an Eskimo canoe," Fritz said. "It is made of skins stretched over a light frame with an opening in the middle for the canoeist. I have read that the Eskimos carry their kayaks on their shoulders when they reach land."

"A boat such as that would be very useful," I said. "I think we should start building one at once."

By the end of the day we had completed the framework. The two sides were made from strips of whalebone and bamboo canes with moss and rushes woven in to form the skeleton. We coated the inside with a layer of gum and stretched two large, seal skins over the shell of the kayak. We sewed them together down the middle and at each end. Then we smeared melted rubber all over the outside of the vessel to make it waterproof.

I made a bamboo paddle with a blade at both ends and Elizabeth made Fritz an airtight life-jacket which covered him from tip to toe. The waterproof suit could be inflated with air by blowing into a tube at the front. We all laughed out loud when we first saw Fritz in his suit because he looked so funny in it. Fritz, however, simply marched into the water and began swimming towards Shark Island. We followed in the canoe and stepped ashore just as Fritz arrived. When Fritz removed his jacket we were delighted to find that not one drop of water had seeped through. Elizabeth agreed to make suits for the rest of us.

We made a tour of the island and were pleased to see that the antelope, birds and rabbits were all doing well in their new home. We decided to build ourselves a small fortress on Shark Island where we could take refuge from any enemy attack. It was an incredibly

difficult project which took us two months to complete. We moved our two cannon to the island and hauled them up on to a rock commanding the country around *Felsenheim* and the open sea beyond. We constructed a watch-tower and, when all was ready, we hoisted the Swiss flag to the top of a pole and fired the cannon in salute.

One day when Fritz was out with the kayak he was caught in the strong current at the mouth of Jackal River and swept out to sea. We searched for hours and eventually found him safe on a rock. By his side was a huge walrus which he had killed with a harpoon. Fritz cut off its head and when he got home he stuffed it and fixed it to the front of the kayak which, he now informed us, was to be known as "The Walrus".

Chapter 14
Pearl Bay: A Strange Message

So ten years rolled by. My sons grew up strong and healthy and now they were fine young men; Fritz was twenty-five years old, Jack, twenty-three, Ernest, twenty-one and Francis, just sixteen. During our time on the island they had become very independent and often went out alone to hunt or explore.

One day Fritz set out before dawn and was gone the whole day. It was getting quite dark when Elizabeth came up to me and said tearfully,

"I am becoming more and more worried about Fritz. Please go and look for him."

So Jack, Ernest, Francis and I set out for Shark Island in the canoe. From the watch-tower we could see for miles but we saw nothing at first. Then I raised the telescope to my eye and there on the horizon I could just make out Fritz, who was paddling slowly towards us.

When his kayak was beached I said,

"You are safe, thank heaven. But what a terrible fright you gave us, Fritz. Where have you been all this time?"

"I'm sorry I went off without your permission, Father, but as you can see, I am all right. I've been exploring the area beyond the spot where I killed the walrus," said Fritz. "And," he added, mysteriously, "I have made one marvellous discovery and one very puzzling one indeed!"

We listened intently as Fritz began his story.

"I sailed past our sunken ship and round a rocky headland where I saw hundreds of walruses, sea-lions and sea-elephants all basking in the sun. I was afraid that these enormous sea-animals might overturn my kayak so I paddled on as fast as I could. Suddenly, in front of me there was a huge, rocky archway which led into a vast cave and out into a magnificent bay. I steered my way through to the calm, clear waters of the bay and there found scores of giant oysters lying on the sea bed. I gathered some with my boat-hook and threw them on to the sand but when I opened them I was disappointed to find that the flesh was too coarse to eat. However, while I was cleaning one of the shells my knife struck something hard and I prised out a pearl. I found beautiful pearls in the rest of the oysters too and they are all here in this box."

Fritz handed me the box of pearls and I examined each one.

"You have made a wonderful discovery, Fritz, for these are extremely valuable pearls. We will gather more of them soon," I said.

Then Fritz drew a small piece of cloth from his pocket and said,

"Look, Father, I found this note tied to the leg of a sea-gull who was pecking at the oyster scraps. The message is written in English and reads: 'Please save the poor, shipwrecked sailor on the smoking rock.'"

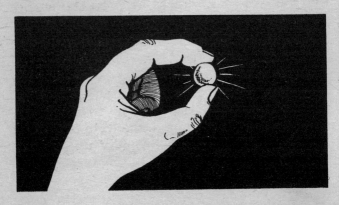

Chapter 15
Jenny Montrose

I took the note from Fritz and read it over and over again for it was hard to believe that we were no longer alone on the island. Finally, I spoke,

"We must find the poor, unfortunate sailor stranded on the 'smoking rock'," I said.

"We could send him a message," Fritz suggested. "The sea-gull that carried the note to me is here in a sack."

With that, he fetched the bird from the kayak and held it in his arms while I wrote

on the reverse side of the cloth: 'Trust in God. Help is at hand.'

I quickly tied the cloth to one of the sea-gull's legs and when Fritz released the bird it flew off westward.

We spent the next day preparing our equipment for the pearl-fishing expedition. We set off as soon as the wind was favourable. Fritz took the lead in his kayak; Jack and Knips junior, the son of our first tame monkey, sailed with him; Ernest and I followed in the canoe with Flora and Turk, our two faithful dogs. We soon rounded the headland and sailed on through the magnificent archway and out into the bay beyond. The beauty of it left us breathless and we gazed in wonder at the countless beds of giant oysters where Fritz had found his pearls. We named this lovely place the Bay of Pearls. As it was late, we decided to rest for the night and begin our pearl-fishing early

the next day. At dawn, we rowed to the oyster beds where with the aid of the special equipment we had prepared at *Felsenheim* – long poles, rakes, hooks and nets – we soon gathered a mass of oysters. To our delight we found that each one contained a precious, gleaming pearl.

That evening, as we rested by the camp-fire after supper, we heard a terrifying roar echo from the woods nearby. Then the roaring came nearer and, suddenly, a huge lion sprang out and crouched before us, ready to attack. Before I could raise my gun we heard a single shot and the lion fell dead on the ground.

"Good shooting, Fritz!" cried Ernest. "You shot him straight through the heart and saved us from a certain death!"

But Fritz had no time to respond for, seconds later, a lioness came into view. She moved quickly towards the body of her dead

mate. She smelled his blood, licked his fur and suddenly gave a series of angry, piercing cries as she turned ferociously on us.

Fritz fired a second shot which shattered the lioness's right paw. Our dogs hurled themselves upon her and, in the fearsome fight that followed, our beloved Flora received a fatal wound to the chest. I managed to thrust my knife into the throat of the lioness and she too fell dead on the ground.

"Poor Flora!" cried Fritz. "She did for us tonight just what Grizzle did with the boa all those years ago."

Sadly, we prepared a grave for our brave pet. My sons lowered her into the grave and we held a torchlight funeral in her honour. We fixed a tombstone to mark the spot where she lay buried and then Ernest scratched the following words on the stone:

Here lies
FLORA
A Dog of True Courage and Devotion who,
at the Moment of Victory, died under the
Claws of a Murderous Lioness.

Early next morning we skinned the lions
and set sail for *Felsenheim*. Fritz led the
way in his kayak while Ernest, Jack and I
steered the canoe. When we were safely
through the rocky archway Fritz paddled up
and handed me a note. Then, to my astonishment, he shot off in the opposite direction
and disappeared behind some jagged rocks.
I read Fritz's note. In it he told me he had
gone in search of the shipwrecked sailor.
Concerned as I was for Fritz's safety, I
decided to continue our journey home for
we had been away several days and I knew
that Elizabeth and Francis would be worried
about us. Their joy at our return was marred

by Fritz's absence and the news of Flora's death. We waited anxiously for five days. There was still no sign of Fritz so we all set off in the little sailing-boat to find him. As we sailed along the coast towards Pearl Bay, Ernest suddenly cried out in terror and pointed to a small canoe in the distance.

"Look!" he yelled. "I see a man! A savage! And he's coming towards us!"

We were very frightened. As the stranger drew near I called out to him in the Malay tongue but he said nothing. Then Jack tried English. He shouted a few well-known sailing expressions that would be familiar to anyone who had ever been on board ship. To our relief the savage gave a friendly wave with the green branch in his hand and then he paddled up to us. We saw at once that the painted savage was none other than our own, dear Fritz! Once the excitement had died down we asked him many questions. He told

us that he had disguised himself as a savage to frighten away any enemies he might meet. Then he said,

"I have found the shipwrecked sailor."

While the others were discussing this exciting news, Fritz took me aside and said in a whisper,

"Father, the sailor is a girl. Her name is Jenny. She would like to come and live with us but she doesn't want anyone except you and Mother to know she is a girl. Can we go and fetch her now?"

I agreed at once. Fritz set off in the kayak and we followed close behind. He stopped at a nearby island and we quickly secured our boats to a tree. Fritz ran towards a small clearing where we could see a fire burning in front of a little hut.

"Hello," Fritz called in a loud voice.

We heard a slight rustle then a handsome,

young sailor jumped down from a nearby tree.

"Hello. I am Sir Edward Montrose," said the stranger.

Chapter 16
A Sad Parting

It was so long since we had seen another human being that we simply stood and stared at the young sailor in complete silence. Eventually, Fritz took the sailor by the hand and led her to us.

"Mother, Father, Jack, Ernest, Francis," he said, "I would like you to meet our new friend, Sir Edward Montrose."

We all shook hands and welcomed the stranger into our family. It was an emotional moment for everyone. The young sailor burst into tears and ran into Elizabeth's arms.

"You are all so kind, I will never be able to thank you enough!"

After supper, Elizabeth conducted the weary sailor to a comfortable bed on our sailing-boat. We, however, stayed by the fire and listened to Fritz's account of his expedition. During the telling of his story he became so excited that he called our new friend Jenny instead of Sir Edward.

"Jenny!" his brothers cried in surprise. "Are you telling us that the sailor you rescued is a girl?"

"She is indeed," Fritz replied. "She pretended to be a boy because she has only sailors' clothes to wear."

Next morning we were all very cheerful. My sons had gained a sister, Elizabeth and I, a beautiful new daughter. We returned to *Felsenheim* where Elizabeth prepared a magnificent supper in celebration of Jenny's arrival.

Later that evening Jenny told us the story of her life.

"I was born in England. When I was seven years old my mother died so I went to India to join my father, Sir William Montrose, who was an officer in the British Army. When I was seventeen my father was ordered to return to England with his regiment. Army regulations prevented me from travelling on the troop-ship with him so I sailed on another vessel. After days at sea a dreadful storm arose and we were shipwrecked. I was knocked unconscious and when I came to I found myself alone on a small island. Fortunately, my father had taught me how to hunt and fish so I was never without food. I tamed a cormorant and trained it to bring me the fish it caught. I also caught birds and rabbits. I built myself a little hut and I kept a fire burning day and night in order to attract the attention of any passing ship. Three years

went by. Then Fritz found me and now I am safe with my new family."

Jenny was such a delightful girl that within days we felt she must always have been a part of our lives. We spent many happy weeks showing Jenny all that we had accomplished on our island. Then one day Jack and Fritz took a trip to Shark Island to check on the fortress. They fired two shots from the cannon and, to their amazement, they heard several cannon shots fired in reply. They rushed home to tell me about it.

"I don't know what to think," I said. "The shots could have come from a European ship but it is also possible that they were fired by pirates."

We made our way to the beach and scanned the bay. There, to our right, lying close to the shore, was a splendid, European ship with the English flag flying from her mainmast. Still fearing a trick and uncertain of the ship's identity, we hid behind rocks. We watched some sailors come ashore and set up camp for dinner. Two sentries stood guard. After a while we showed ourselves but we kept our distance.

"Ahoy there!" we cried. "Englishmen, ahoy!"

There was no answer; our strange clothes and tanned skins must have convinced them we were savages!

"We must make ourselves known to the captain at once," said Elizabeth. "We will sail out to the ship with gifts for him and his men."

The captain of the "Unicorn", Captain Littleton, greeted us very warmly indeed, no doubt relieved to see we were not savages after all. He escorted us to his cabin for a glass of wine and to hear our story. I told him as quickly as I could. To our surprise, he knew Colonel Montrose and was able to confirm that Jenny's father was alive. Then the captain introduced us to Mr Wolston, his wife and their two daughters, an English family who were passengers on the ship. We invited the Wolstons to visit our home. Elizabeth prepared a special dinner for them and then insisted that they spend the night at *Felsenheim*.

Next morning Mr Wolston told me that he and his family so admired our way of life that they wished to remain on the island. I agreed at once for I was anxious to establish a permanent colony. Elizabeth and I had already made up our minds to stay but we felt that our sons should decide for themselves whether to leave on the "Unicorn" or to stay on the island forever. I called a family meeting to discuss the matter. Ernest and Jack said they had no desire to leave for they were happy and content on the island. For a while Fritz was silent, then he

told us that both he and Francis wished to return to Europe together.

The "Unicorn" stayed at anchor in the bay for seven more days. During that time we carefully packed and loaded all the ivory, pearls, furs and spices that we had collected over the years. Our sons would sell these precious goods in Europe to provide for their future.

At dawn on the eighth day a shot from the cannon announced that the ship was ready to depart. Sadly, we said our good-byes, tenderly embracing Fritz, Francis and Jenny for the last time.

"Good-bye, dear loved-ones. May God bless you and keep you safe," we whispered softly.

The "Unicorn" weighed anchor and we watched her sail out across the bay and dis-appear over the horizon, taking with her our last farewell to Europe and dear Switzerland, our own, beloved, native land.